Ganesha's Mousecapade

by Swamini Supriyananda

C·H·I·N·M·A·Y·A B·A·L·A K·A·T·H·A

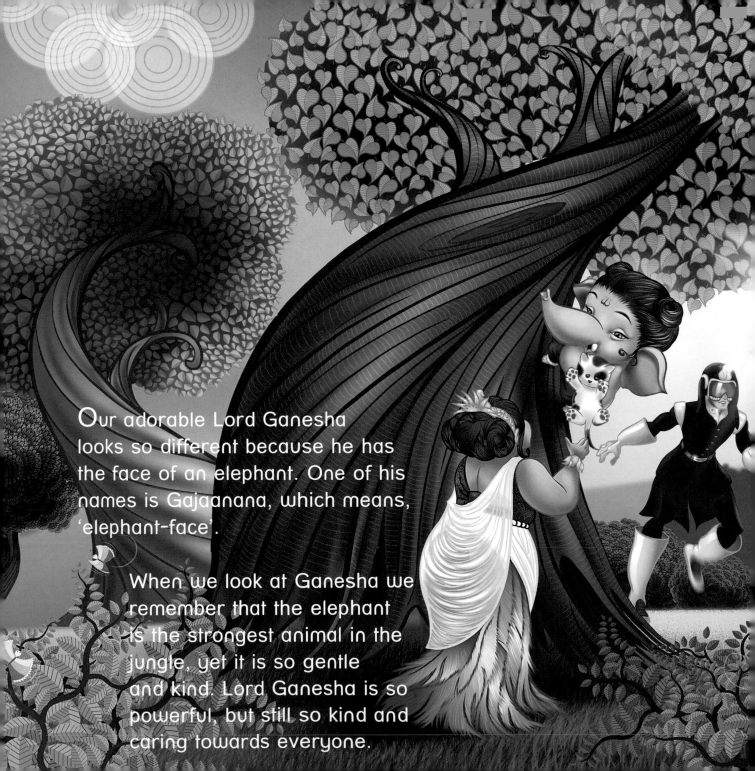

Our adorable Lord Ganesha looks so different because he has the face of an elephant. One of his names is Gajaanana, which means, 'elephant-face'.

When we look at Ganesha we remember that the elephant is the strongest animal in the jungle, yet it is so gentle and kind. Lord Ganesha is so powerful, but still so kind and caring towards everyone.

There was another person with an elephant head, but he was very very very different from magnificent Ganesha.

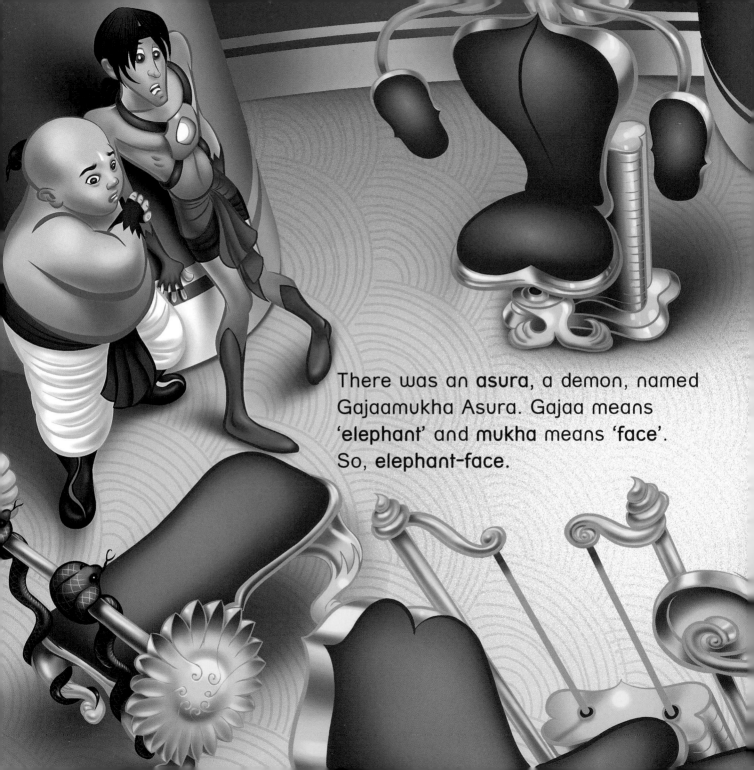

There was an **asura**, a demon, named Gajaamukha Asura. Gajaa means 'elephant' and **mukha** means 'face'. So, elephant-face.

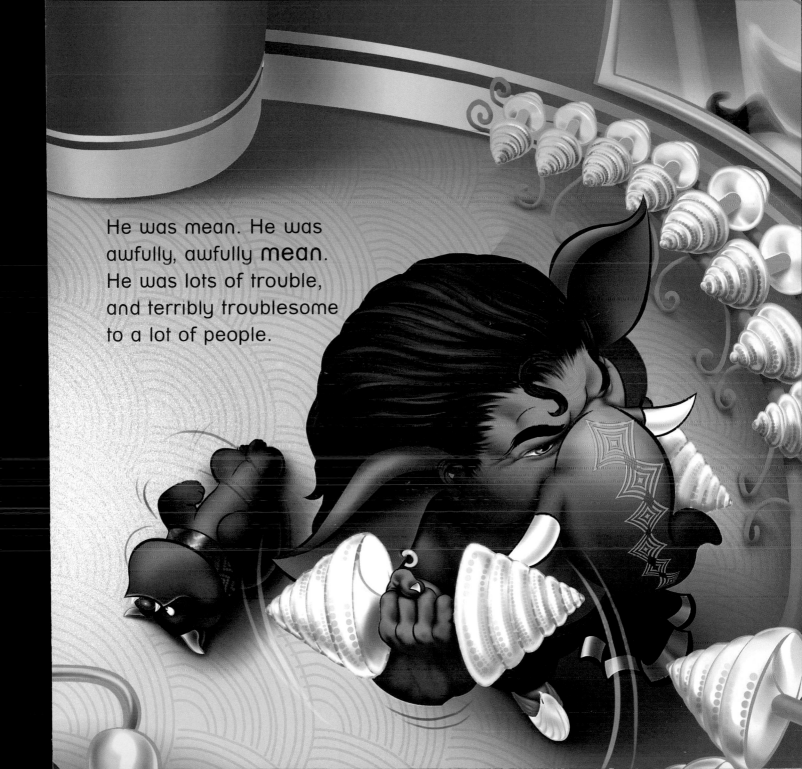

He was mean. He was awfully, awfully **mean**. He was lots of trouble, and terribly troublesome to a lot of people.

One day Gajaamukha was walking through the city. He overheard two people talking.

"How strange! Gajaamukha Asura has the face of an elephant, just like Ganesha. But he is nothing like Ganesha at all," said the first person.

"Yes, you are right, Gajaamukha has a heart that is angry, a tongue that is nasty and a face that is scowling," said the second person.

"But Ganesha always has a cute little smile on his chubby little face. He has a happy little sparkle in his **big**, brown eyes.

He has a song in his heart and kindness in his words," said the first person.

"Everyone loves joyful little Ganesha and wants to see his beautiful, beaming face," added the second person, "but no one wants to see Gajaamukha's long and grumpy face . . ."

"Who dares speak about me like that?"
thundered angry Gajaamukha.

A very angry, very mean Gajaamukha walked
towards the two men. He held up his hand
and formed a fist to hit them.

The men started running.
They ran as fast as they could.

They huffed and they puffed.
They skittered and they scattered.

They had to get away.
Far. . . far away from Gajaamukha.

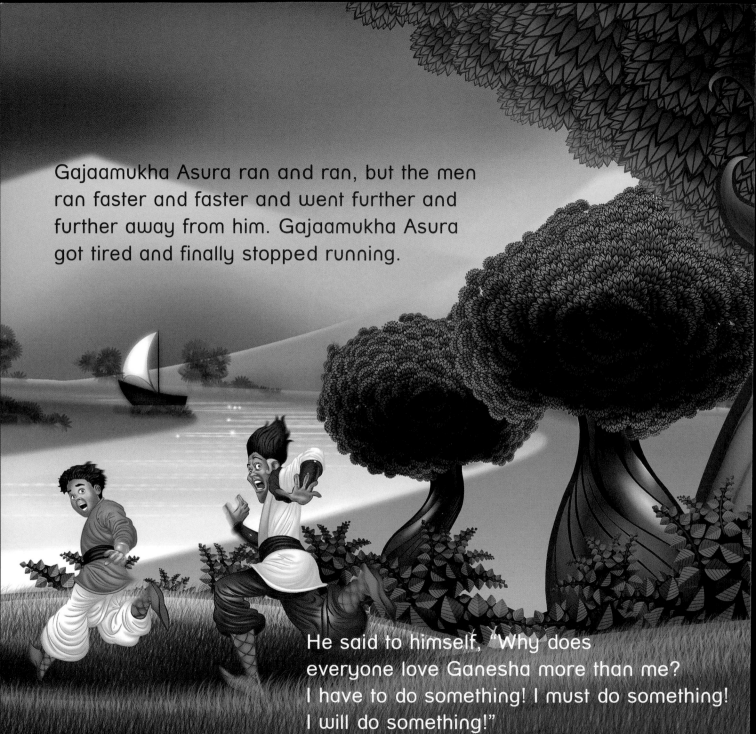

Gajaamukha Asura ran and ran, but the men ran faster and faster and went further and further away from him. Gajaamukha Asura got tired and finally stopped running.

He said to himself, "Why does everyone love Ganesha more than me? I have to do something! I must do something! I will do something!"

He thought about it for a while. "Ah! I will fight Ganesha and beat him. Then everyone will know that I am better. No, they will know that I am the best! The one and only Gajaamukha, elephant-face."

Gajaamukha Asura went up to Mount Kailash — a very **tall**, very **high**, very **big** mountain where chubby little Ganesha lived with his family.

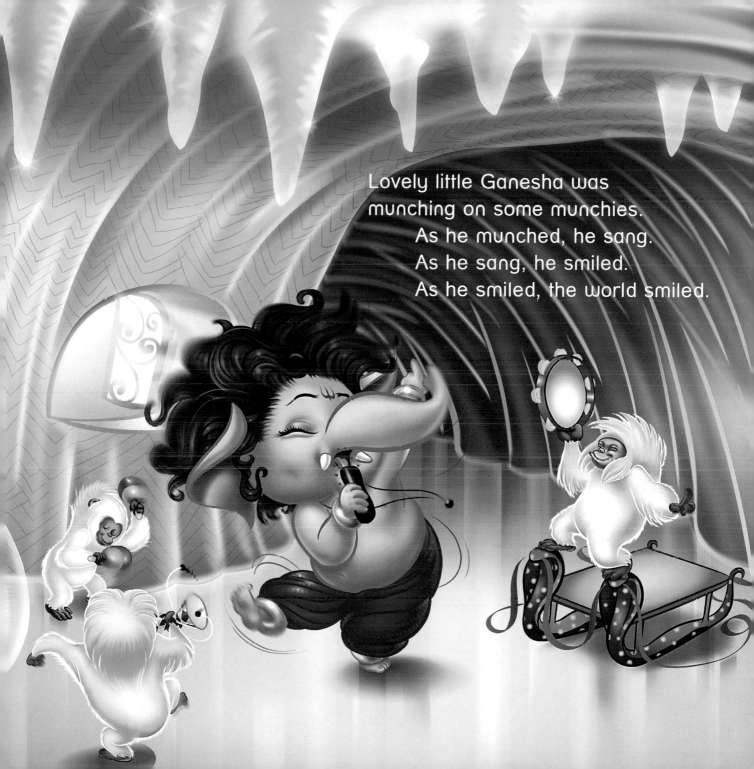

Lovely little Ganesha was
munching on some munchies.
As he munched, he sang.
As he sang, he smiled.
As he smiled, the world smiled.

Gajaamukha stood in Ganesha's beautiful garden and yelled, "Ganesha, come out! Come out and fight with me!" The asura shouted a dreadfully loud shout. He screamed an especially angry scream.

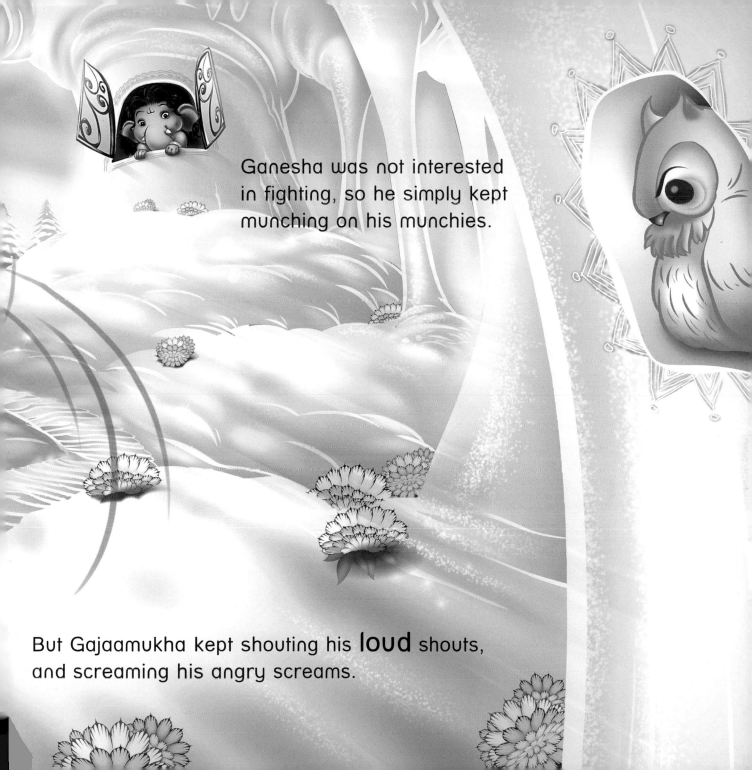

Ganesha was not interested in fighting, so he simply kept munching on his munchies.

But Gajaamukha kept shouting his **loud** shouts, and screaming his angry screams.

The ever-peaceful Lord Shiva, Ganesha's dad,
grew tired of all the shouting and screaming.

In a deep, strong voice, he said, "Ganesha,
are you going to take care of this matter or shall I?"

So the chubby little Ganesha went out to face the mean and nasty Gajaamukha.

Smart little Ganesha had a peaceful little smile.
He walked calmly and gently, but quickly and carefully.
He didn't really want to fight with Gajaamukha,
but he always does what is best for everyone.

Gajaamukha started flexing
his muscles, clenching his
hands and scowling
his scowl.

Ganesha pulled out his sharp tusk and with his strong, chubby little hand...

...whoosh!

he threw it at Gajaamukha.

Gajaamuhka fell on the ground with a great big THUD.

"HUH? But . . . how . . .
Huh? What happened?!"
said Gajaamukha Asura.

"Hmm, now what shall we do with you?" said Ganesha. He put his chubby little hand on his chubby little chin, and looked up thoughtfully.

Gajaamuhka tried to get up. And then he fell down again. He realised that Ganesha was much stronger and much wiser than he. He knew now that he was wrong to always be so mean and troublesome.

Gajaamuhka pleaded: "I am sorry. So very **very** sorry.

I was angry and cruel, but you are kind and helpful. Please do not hurt me. Please help me to be more like you, dear Ganesha."

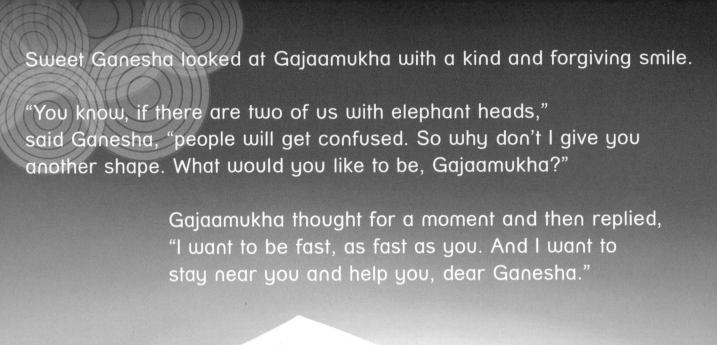

Sweet Ganesha looked at Gajaamukha with a kind and forgiving smile.

"You know, if there are two of us with elephant heads,"
said Ganesha, "people will get confused. So why don't I give you
another shape. What would you like to be, Gajaamukha?"

Gajaamukha thought for a moment and then replied,
"I want to be fast, as fast as you. And I want to
stay near you and help you, dear Ganesha."

Cute little Ganesha snapped his chubby little fingers. "I got it, I'll turn you into a mouse! My very own little mouse-mobile, to take me wherever I want to go."

Gajaamukha Asura smiled and agreed. He would be the fastest mouse ever and always with the kind and helpful Lord Ganesha.

Then, without a moment's delay, Ganesha turned Gajaamukha into a tiny, grey mouse.

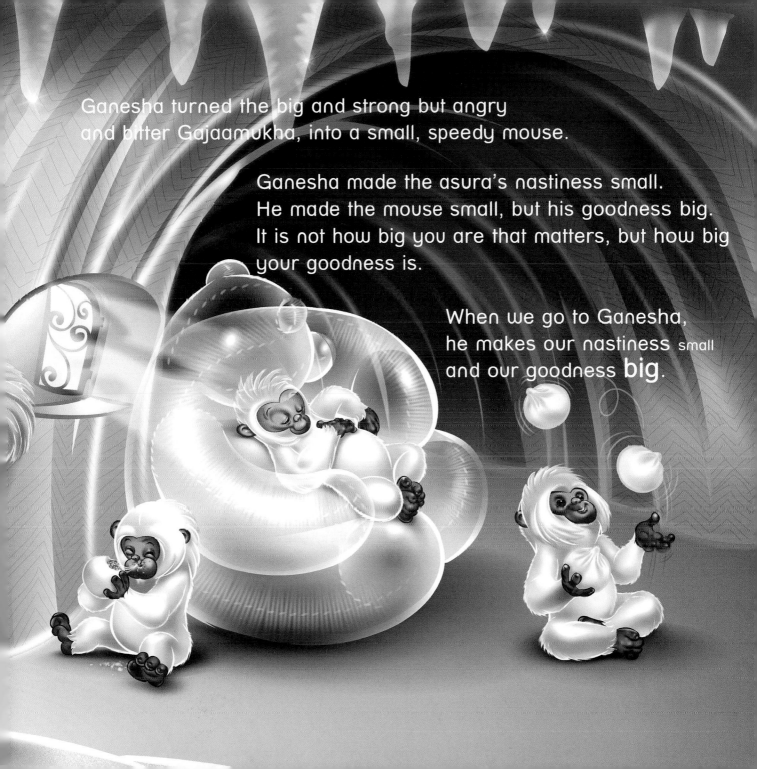

Ganesha turned the big and strong but angry and bitter Gajaamukha, into a small, speedy mouse.

Ganesha made the asura's nastiness small.
He made the mouse small, but his goodness big.
It is not how big you are that matters, but how big your goodness is.

When we go to Ganesha,
he makes our nastiness small
and our goodness big.

Nobody liked to see Gajaamukha Asura.
They always ran away from him.
But these days whenever they see
a speedy little mouse, people rush
to see if Ganesha is around.

Do people like to see you around?
How big is your goodness?

And how much **bigger** can your goodness get?